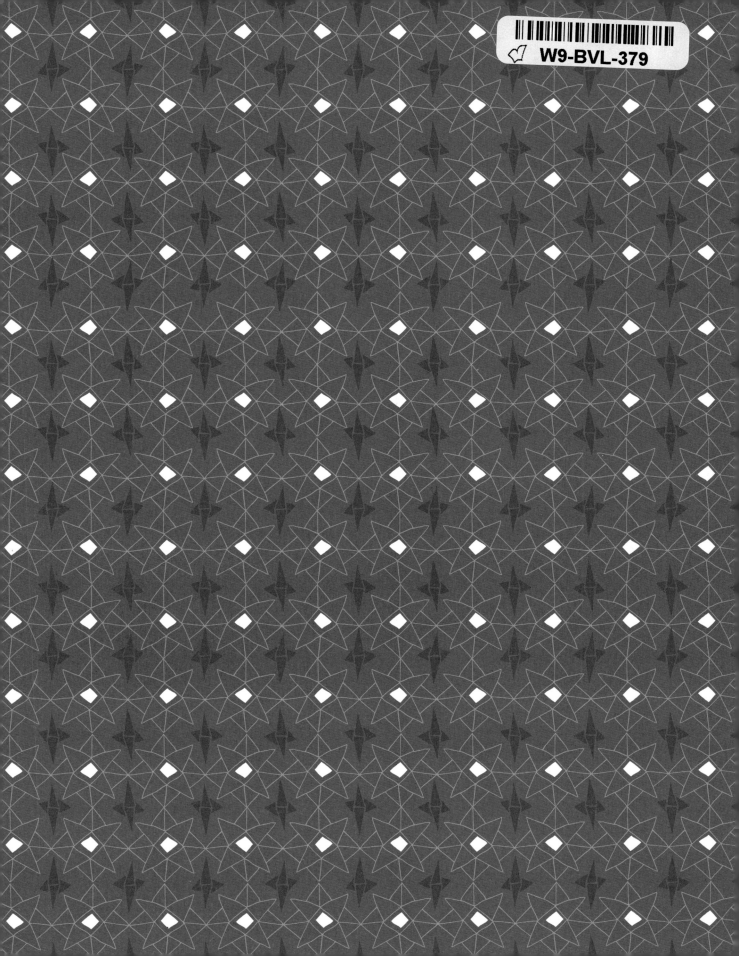

Hank and Gertie came west in a covered wagon. One dry, dusty day the wagon train stopped by a stream.

"We'll have lunch here and water the animals," the wagon master said.

Hank wanted to go exploring. Gertie wanted to pick wildflowers.

"Don't get lost," their Ma said. "We can't stop to look for you."

"We won't!" said Hank. "I'll break off pieces of biscuit as we go. We'll make a trail to follow back when we're done."

"Are you sure you can find our way back?" Gertie asked Hank as they followed the twists and turns of the stream into a canyon.

"Sure, I'm sure!" Hank said, crumbling the biscuit. "Just follow the crumbs."

But when they turned around, there were no crumbs.
Birds had eaten them. Now they truly were lost.

Hank and Gertie wandered through the canyon until they came upon a cabin. The black logs reminded Hank of something, so he tore off a piece

"It's not wood!" Hank said, chewing. "Taste it."

"Licorice!" Gertie exclaimed.

"And these shingles…" Hank broke a chunk off and popped it in his mouth. "They're rock candy!"

"It's a candy cabin!" Gertie hollered. She broke some off for herself.

Suddenly they heard a voice:

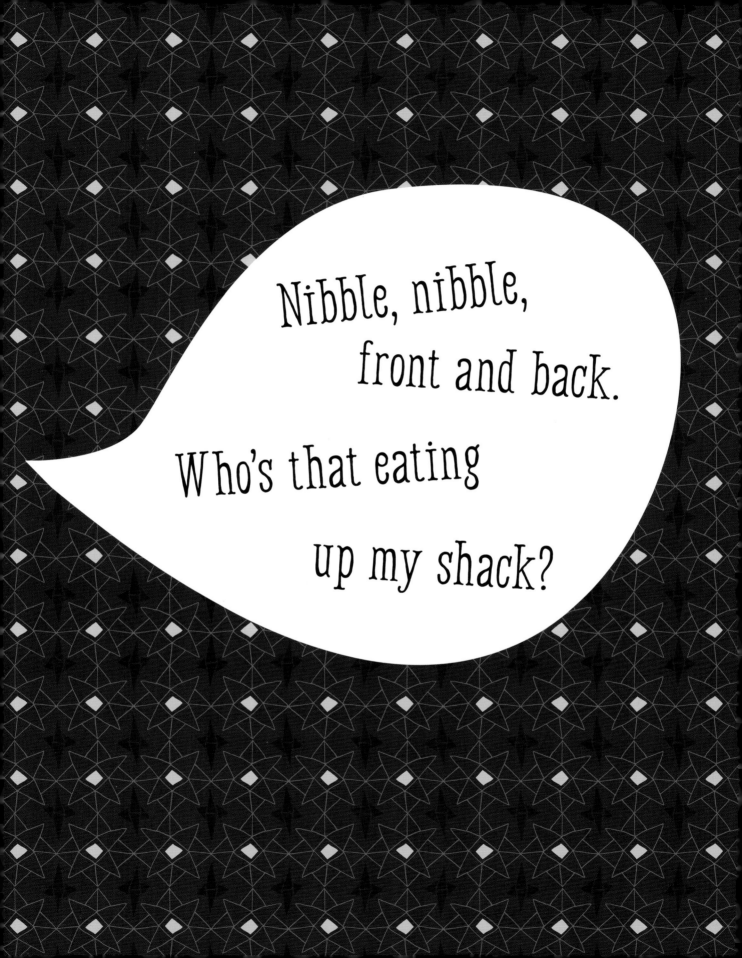

There stood the scariest woman Hank and Gertie ever saw. She had a face like old rawhide. Her clothes were odds and ends left behind on the trail:

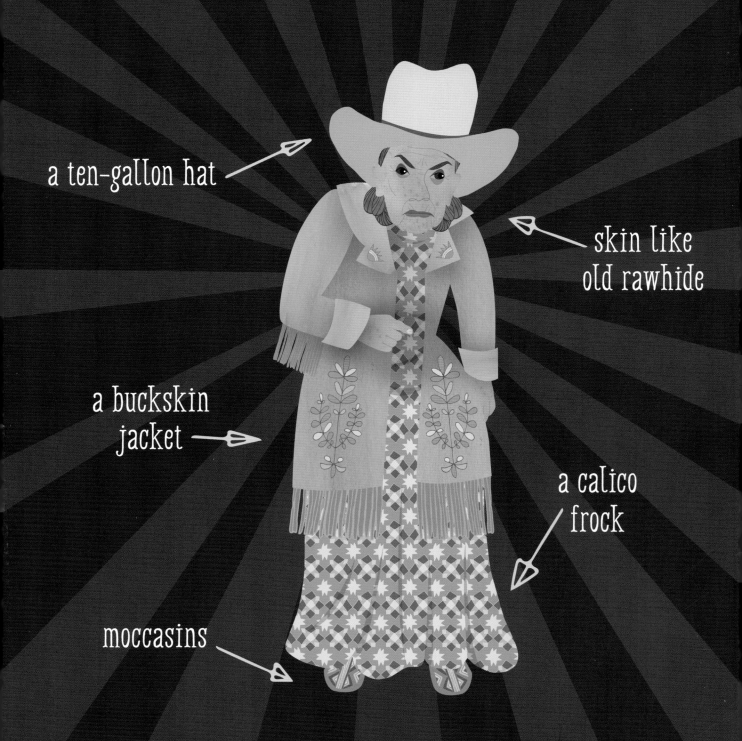

a ten-gallon hat

skin like old rawhide

a buckskin jacket

a calico frock

moccasins

Hank and Gertie were too scared to run. Where could they run to?

"Let us go," Hank pleaded. "We have to get back to Ma and the wagon train."

"Sorry," said Gertie. "We didn't mean to eat your cabin, Miss…"

"Call me Aunt Caroline. And it's too late for sorry. Anyway, your wagon train is long gone. You'll be staying with me awhile. What do you say to that?"

"I don't like it at all," said Gertie.

"Can we have more candy?" asked Hank.

"Eat much as you like," Aunt Caroline told Hank. "As for you…" She dragged Gertie to the corral. In it was nothing but a big pile of rocks and an old wash kettle.

"Don't try to run away," Aunt Caroline told Gertie as she shackled an iron ball and chain to her ankle. "That kettle flies. I'll find you no matter where you run. And when I do…"

Gertie was too scared to even cry.

Meanwhile, Hank was having the time of his life. Aunt Caroline sat him down at the dinner table and stuffed him with:

pumpkin pie

applesauce

fried chicken

stewed prunes

coffee cake

boiled ham

lemonade

hot chocolate

dried figs

store cheese

Gertie got no dinner at all.

That night Hank slept on a soft feather bed.
In the morning Aunt Caroline served him
fried eggs, bacon, and doughnuts for breakfast.

Gertie slept on the hard ground in the corral. Aunt Caroline brought her cornbread and beans for breakfast.

Four beans. Six crumbs of cornbread.

Before Gertie could even finish eating, Aunt Caroline dragged her to the rock pile.

"I want these rocks moved from here to there. When you're done, move 'em back again." Aunt Caroline jumped in her kettle and flew away.

Poor Gertie lugged rocks from one end of the corral to the other, dragging the iron ball behind. The work never ended.

Hank came by to check on her. He brought molasses cookies.

"This sure beats eating hardtack and beans," he said. "Aunt Caroline's nice. I like her."

"You wouldn't like her if she made you haul rocks all day," muttered Gertie as Hank walked back to the cabin.

That night Aunt Caroline and Hank had a party. They ate:

grilled oysters

onion puffs

hoecakes and biscuits

buffalo hump

wild turkey

duff pudding with maple cream sauce

After dessert, Aunt Caroline sat down at the piano. They sang
"Oh, Susannah," "Sweet Betsy From Pike," and lots of other songs.
Afterward, Hank had pleasant dreams in his feather bed.

Gertie shivered in the corral. She sure didn't feel like singing. This went on for days. Gertie got thinner and thinner while Hank grew fatter and fatter.

"You'll bust out of your clothes if you keep eating," Gertie told him.

"Who cares?" said Hank. "Aunt Caroline promised me fine new clothes. I'm gonna look like a king."

Gertie wondered, What was the matter with Hank? Couldn't he see what was happening?

Unless… maybe Aunt Caroline wasn't just a mean old lady. Maybe she was a witch and she put a spell on Hank. But why?

Suddenly, Gertie noticed two buzzards overhead. "Poor girl!" she heard one say.

"I feel sorrier for the boy," the other buzzard said.

Gertie listened closely. You know you're in trouble when buzzards feel sorry for you.

"She'll fire up the smoker soon," the first buzzard said. "That boy'll make good barbecue."

"Think she'll barbecue the girl?"

"Naw! She'll just work her till she drops. Aunt Caroline doesn't like skinny little heifers."

"But we do!" The buzzards laughed as they flew off.

spittin' mad

angry

frustrated

irked

calm

Gertie felt scared but also spittin' mad.
No witch was gonna barbecue her
brother! Not if she could help it.

Aunt Caroline flew in that evening. Her kettle was loaded with mesquite logs. "What're those for?" Gertie asked.

"Gonna fire up my smoker. Fixin' to make me some barbecue," Aunt Caroline said.

The buzzards were right!

Gertie shivered, but she didn't let on.

"Aunt Caroline, may I ask you something?" Gertie asked.

"Sure. Just make it quick," Aunt Caroline said.

"Are you a witch?"

"Of course I'm a witch. Didn't you see me fly on my kettle?"

"Maybe the kettle's magic, not you," Gertie said. "I've never seen you work any magic. Can you, Aunt Caroline?"

"Sure I can! What kind of magic do you want?"

"Could you change one of these boulders into a…" Gertie thought for a minute. "Into a coyote?"

"Easy as pie!" Aunt Caroline snapped her fingers. The biggest boulder turned into a coyote with yellow eyes. "Satisfied?"

"Sorta," Gertie said. "What about you? Can you change yourself into something? Maybe a jackrabbit?"

Aunt Caroline laughed. "You can't trick me, little girl. I'm not changing into a jackrabbit with a coyote looking on."

"Then how about a rattlesnake!" said Gertie, scratching her chin. "You're mean and ugly enough. A rattler would suit you."

Aunt Caroline laughed. "True enough."

She snapped her fingers again.

In an instant she coiled into a rattlesnake. The snake bared its fangs.
"I'm getting tired of your fresh talk," it said. "I'll finish you off now."

That's when the coyote pounced. It grabbed the rattler and trotted away.

Aunt Caroline didn't figure that coyotes eat rattlesnakes. But Gertie had seen a lot on the wagon train—a coyote'll eat just about anything.

Gertie busted the shackle with a rock and freed herself. She ran to fetch Hank. "Where am I? How'd I get so fat?" Hank asked. He really had been under a spell.

"I'll tell you on the way," said Gertie. She shoved him in the kettle and flew off to find the wagon train.

There it was. Right by the stream where they left it.

"You didn't think we'd leave you behind, did you?" said Ma, wrapping them both in a tight hug. "Where've you been?"

"It's a mighty long story," said Gertie.

"Can we eat first? I'm hungry," said Hank.

"And that," said Gertie, "is how it all started…"

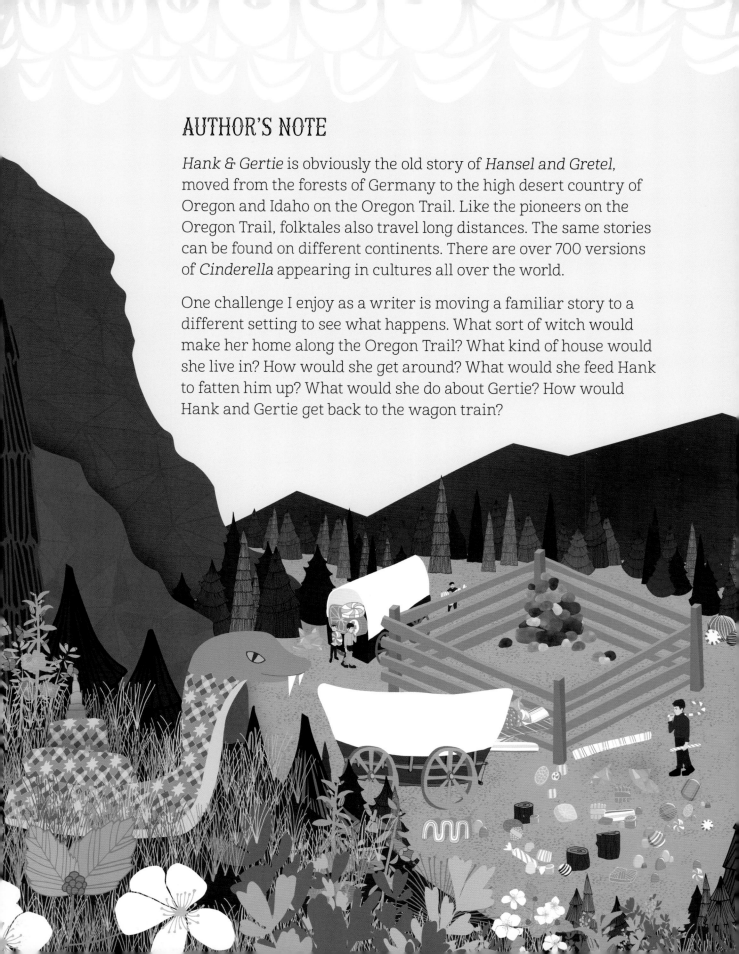

AUTHOR'S NOTE

Hank & Gertie is obviously the old story of *Hansel and Gretel*, moved from the forests of Germany to the high desert country of Oregon and Idaho on the Oregon Trail. Like the pioneers on the Oregon Trail, folktales also travel long distances. The same stories can be found on different continents. There are over 700 versions of *Cinderella* appearing in cultures all over the world.

One challenge I enjoy as a writer is moving a familiar story to a different setting to see what happens. What sort of witch would make her home along the Oregon Trail? What kind of house would she live in? How would she get around? What would she feed Hank to fatten him up? What would she do about Gertie? How would Hank and Gertie get back to the wagon train?

Retelling an old tale is more than just changing a few details. You have to rethink the entire story.

Traveling along the Oregon Trail posed similar challenges. The wagons had to leave late enough in the season for the prairie grass to grow tall enough to feed their horses, oxen, and mules. But not too late, because they needed to be over the mountains before snow blocked the passes. They had to travel light so as not to tire out the animals. They weren't coming back, so precious family possessions had to be left behind. What to bring? What to throw away? So many difficult decisions.

The End of the Oregon Trail Museum in Oregon City, Oregon, has programs and exhibits that fully bring the Oregon Trail experience to life. Visit the museum at 1726 Washington Street in Oregon City or online at www.historicoregoncity.org.

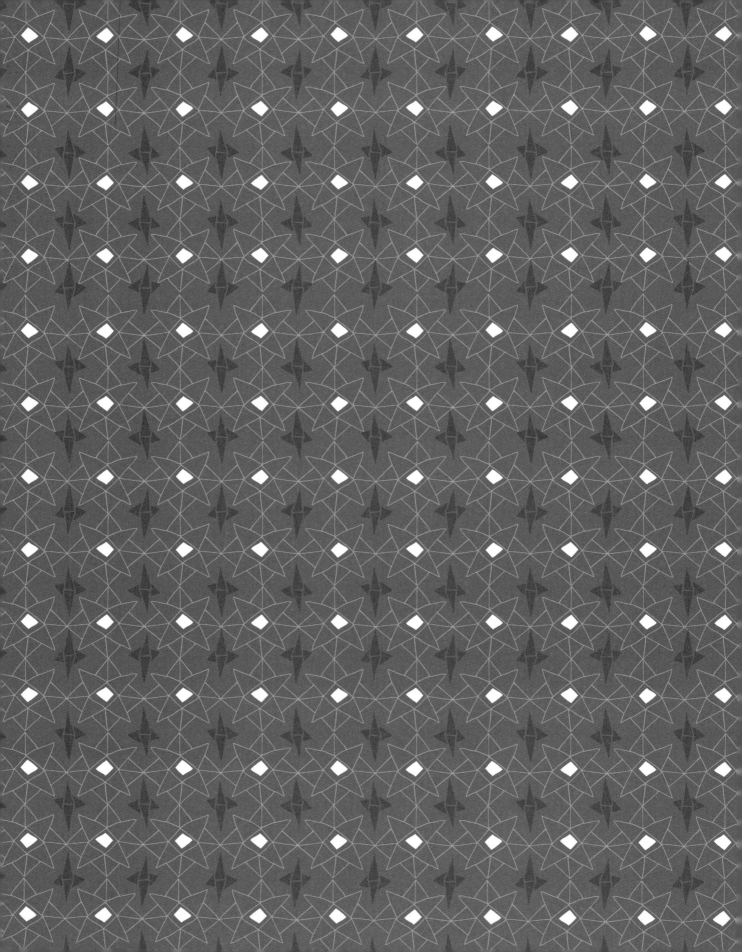